Baby Zebra Helps Out

by Kris Bonnell

The zebras are eating.

3

Mother Zebra is eating, too.

Baby Zebra is looking. What is Baby Zebra looking at?

A lion!

A lion is looking

at the zebras!

Come on!

Come on, Mother Zebra!

Go with Baby Zebra!

Mother Zebra is running with Baby Zebra.

All the zebras are running with Baby Zebra.

The zebras are safe.

Good job, Baby Zebra.